University of Minnesota Press
Minneapolis • London

# ...and Oona

Jacqueline Briggs Martin
Illustrations by Larry Day

Oona:

short legs, big round chest, flat feet—
legs for waddling, not running.

Bim, Bam, Bop:

long legs, long necks, fast feet—

legs for running, not waddling.

When the ducks went to the pond, it was always
Bim, Bam, Bop

. . . . . . . . . . . and Oona.

Oona never saw the morning pond smooth as glass.

Oona never got the best spot under the willow tree.

One day Oona said to Roy,

"Last is a blot on my life.

I don't feel as big as a duck should feel."

"You're plenty big, Oona," Roy said.

"And you're good with gizmos."

*Gizmos . . .*

Oona hatched a plan—
with an alarm clock from the cows,
a pillow so the others wouldn't hear,
and a tangle of string.

The next morning,

brrrrrring, brrrrrring.

Oona scooted out the barn door.

Bim, Bam, and Bop
stretched, wiggled webbed feet—

*Sound sleep,*
*Deep, deep,*
*Counted sheep—*

Oona, out in front.
FIRST.

Up raced Bim, Bam, Bop—

*Good run.*
*Well done.*
*Such fun!*

So it was
Bim, Bam, Bop

. . . . . . . . . . . and Oona.

"Last just drags me down.
I don't feel as bouncy as a duck
    should feel,"
Oona said to Roy.

"You're plenty bouncy, Oona,"
    Roy said.
"And you're good with gizmos."

Oona poked around the farm for scraps
and built a workout machine.
Bim, Bam, and Bop ran after grasshoppers.
Oona tried speed waddling.

Left leg, right leg.
Left leg, right leg.

One morning she was ready.

But again—it was
Bim, Bam, Bop

. . . . . . . . . . and Oona,
who moped back toward the barn,

tripped into a tumble,

and conked herself with an idea . . .

The next morning
Bim, Bam, and Bop ran for
the pond.

Oona stayed back,
climbed into the basket of a
fab-u-lous (she had to
admit it) gizmo.
A gust of wind grabbed the
sails and up she went.

OOO-hoolie-hoo!

The basket rose—and so did Oona—
flying toward the pond.
"Go, Oona, go!" Roy yelled.

**Whoosh, clang, whoosh.**

Oona—FIRST duck to see
patchwork earth from the clouds,
three tiny Runner ducks,
long scarf of a river, little plop of a pond.

Then Oona pulled a string, tilted and
slipped down the branches of the willow tree.
She sat in the warm sun, listened to the rustling reeds,
and felt just as big as a duck should feel.

The Runner ducks came
breathless down the path.

You're the best.
We're impressed.
One request . . .

Now
some days the Runners go to the pond
and Oona stays back, busy with gizmos;
some days she waddles late to the pond.

But most days,
Bim, Bam, Bop
. . . . . . . . . . and Oona (also Roy)

are headed toward sky,
all along together, **OOO**-hoolie-hoo!

For Jonah, Ella, Evelyn, and Owen—all good with all kinds of gizmos
    —J. B. M.


For Miriam Busch, a creative light
    —L. D.

Published by the University of Minnesota Press
111 Third Avenue South, Suite 290
Minneapolis, MN  55401-2520
http://www.upress.umn.edu

LIBRARY OF CONGRESS CATALOGING-IN-PUBLICATION DATA
Martin, Jacqueline Briggs, author. | Day, Larry, illustrator.
Bim, Bam, Bop . . . and Oona / Jacqueline Briggs Martin; illustrations by Larry Day.
Minneapolis : University of Minnesota Press, 2019.
Summary: Oona is the last duck to the pond every morning, but when her frog friend Roy reminds
    her how gifted she is with gadgets, she gets busy inventing crafty ways to get there first.
LCCN 2018020500 | ISBN 978-1-5179-0395-4 (hc/j)
Classification: LCC PZ7.M363165 Bc 2019 | DDC [E]—dc23
LC record available at  https://lccn.loc.gov/2018020500

Printed in Canada on acid-free paper

The University of Minnesota is an equal-opportunity educator and employer.

24  23  22  21  20  19                    10  9  8  7  6  5  4  3  2  1